Hieroglyphic Alphabet

A	K	U
B	L	V
C	M	W
D	N	X
E	O	Y
F	P	Z
G	Q	CH
H	R	KH
I	S	SH
J	T	

Use this alphabet to decode the hieroglyphics on the cover.

For all the amazing children at
Sandringham Primary School. You're ACE! – CH
For Theodore and Nancy xx – EE

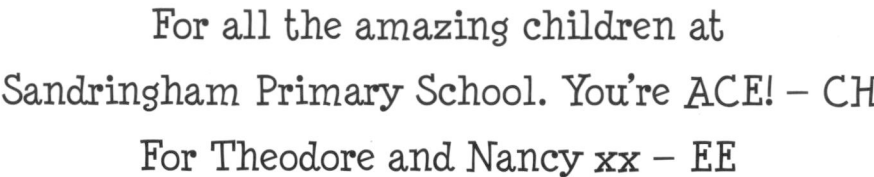

SIMON & SCHUSTER

First published in Great Britain in 2019 by
Simon & Schuster UK Ltd
1st Floor, 222 Gray's Inn Road, London WC1X 8HB
A CBS Company

Text copyright © 2019 Caryl Hart (www.carylhart.com)
Illustrations copyright © 2019 Edward Eaves

The right of Caryl Hart and Edward Eaves to be identified as the
author and illustrator of this work has been asserted by them in
accordance with the Copyright, Designs and Patents Act, 1988

A CIP catalogue record for this book is available from the British Library upon request

PB ISBN: 978-1-4711-6372-2   eBook ISBN: 978-1-4711-6373-9
Printed in China   10 9 8 7 6 5 4 3 2 1

"Well done, Tuti," I say.
"You'll make a great
Pharoah one day."

HOW TO FIND
EGYPTIAN TREASURE

CARYL
HART

ED
EAVES

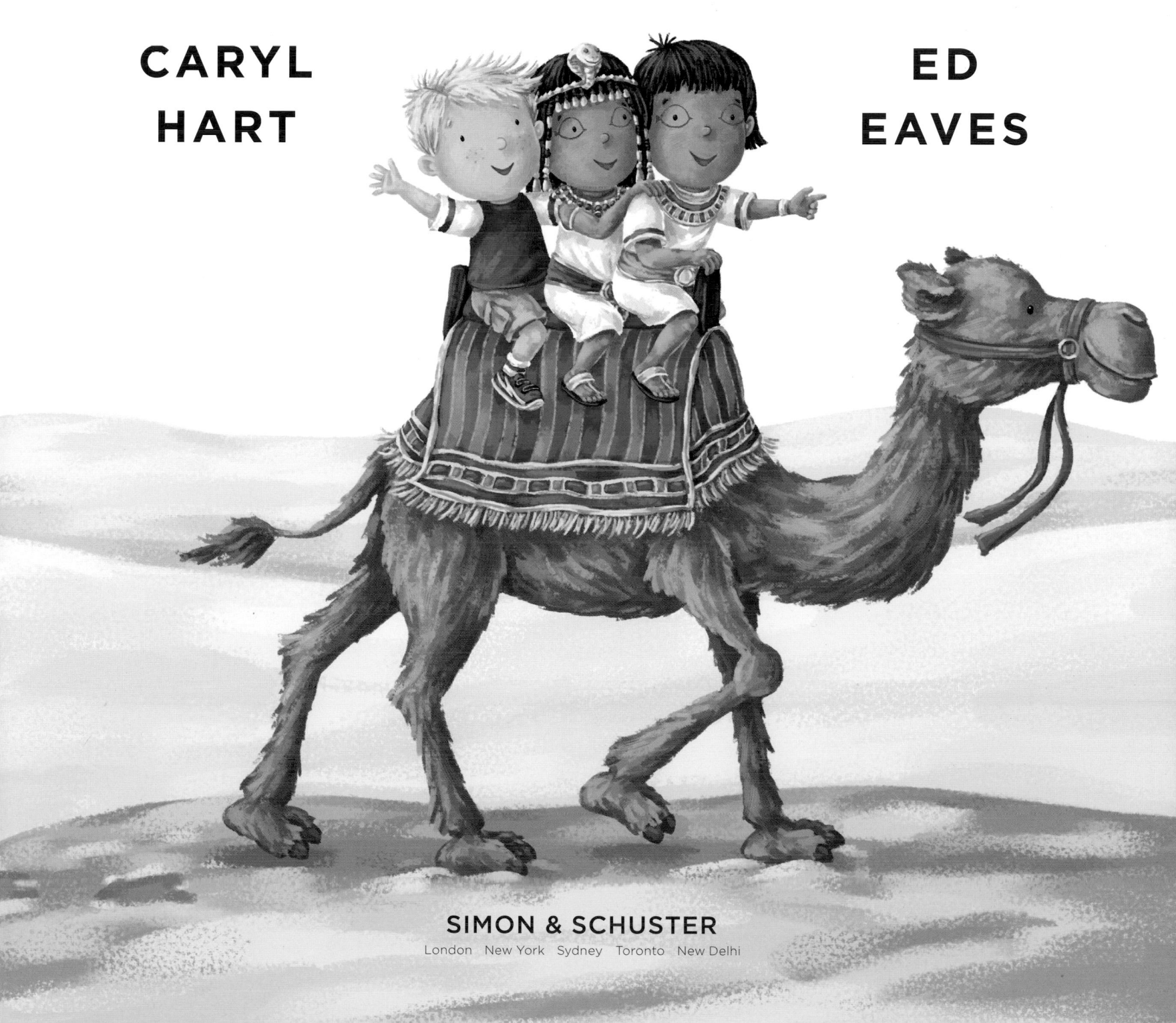

SIMON & SCHUSTER
London   New York   Sydney   Toronto   New Delhi

It's boiling hot outside and I'm having fun digging in the sandpit.

I'm just building a big sandcastle when . . .

"**Albie!**"

It's Mum. "Lunch is ready," she says.

"Are you nearly finished?"

"Almost," I say.

But I don't hear what Mum says next because . . .

... a ferocious wind begins to blow.

It whips up the sand into a terrible tornado.

HEELLPP!

Suddenly someone pulls me into a doorway!

"Great!" says a boy.
"You're just in time."

"My name's Tuti and I'm VERY important," he says.
"One day, I'll be Pharaoh like my dad, but right now,
I'm going exploring. Here —"

He hands me his headdress.

"Put this on and pretend to be me."
"What? WAIT!" I gasp. But Tuti has gone!

Just then, a guard grabs my shoulder.

"Time for your speech, Your Highness!" she says.

On the balcony is a girl.

"Who are you?" she hisses.

"And where's my brother?"

Quickly, I tell her about Tuti.

"I bet he's gone to the catacombs," she exclaims.

"Dad says our great-great-grandad's precious treasure is hidden there. Tuti wants to find it, but we have to stop him."

"Why? It sounds exciting!" I say.

"Some dangerous thieves are looking for the treasure too," says the girl, whose name is Anka. "We've got to find Tuti before they do. Hurry!"

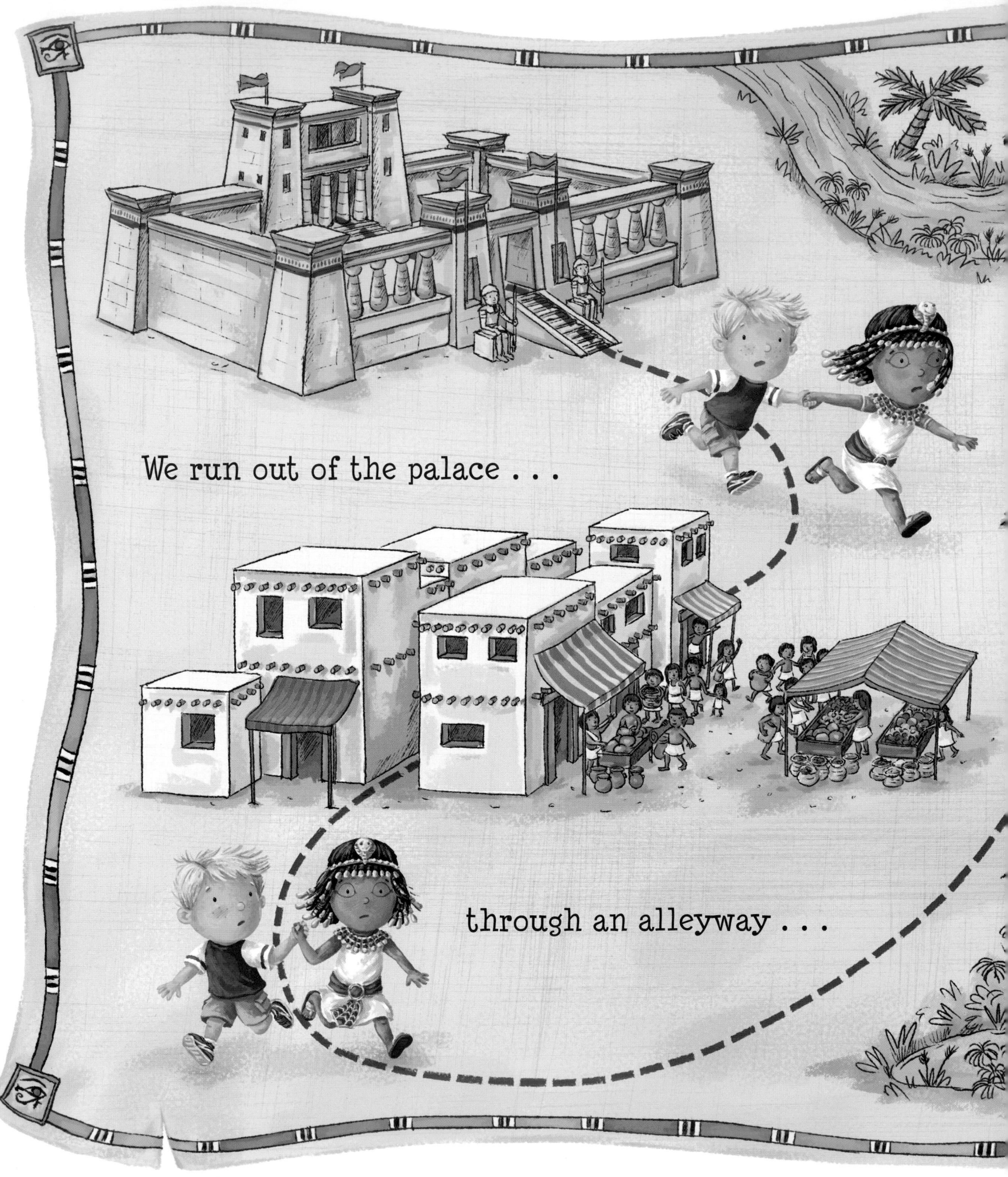

We run out of the palace . . .

through an alleyway . . .

and over the

sand dunes . . .

. . . to a gigantic sphinx.

"Oh no!

I think Tuti's already gone in!" says Anka.

"Gone in?" I ask. "Where?"

Anka pulls at the corner of a stone
and a hidden door grinds open . . .

CREEEAKK!

We tiptoe into the darkness and down a long tunnel . . .

"GOT YOU!"

It's Tuti.

"Haha! Scared you!"
he chuckles.

"Tuti!" cries Anka. "We've got to get out of here!"

"Do we have to?" moans Tuti. "Treasure hunting is fun!"

But as we turn to leave, footsteps echo down the tunnel behind us.

Uh-oh!

We scuttle through the darkness until we reach a huge room.

"Quick!" I say. "In here!" We dive into a chest and huddle together.

Outside, the footsteps get closer. "I know you're in here!" growls a voice. "Come on out!"

I try not to move, but the dust is tickling my nose.

Then . . .

A-A-AAA-CHOOO!

The bottom of the chest falls away and
we shoot down a slippery slope . . . .

WOOAAAHH!

tumble down a pile of rocks . . . .

AAARGGHH!

and land in a clattering heap.

OOF!

But when we look up . . . .

"WOW!" breathes Anka. "Our great-great-grandad's lost treasure! Dad will be so pleased."

"HOORAY!"

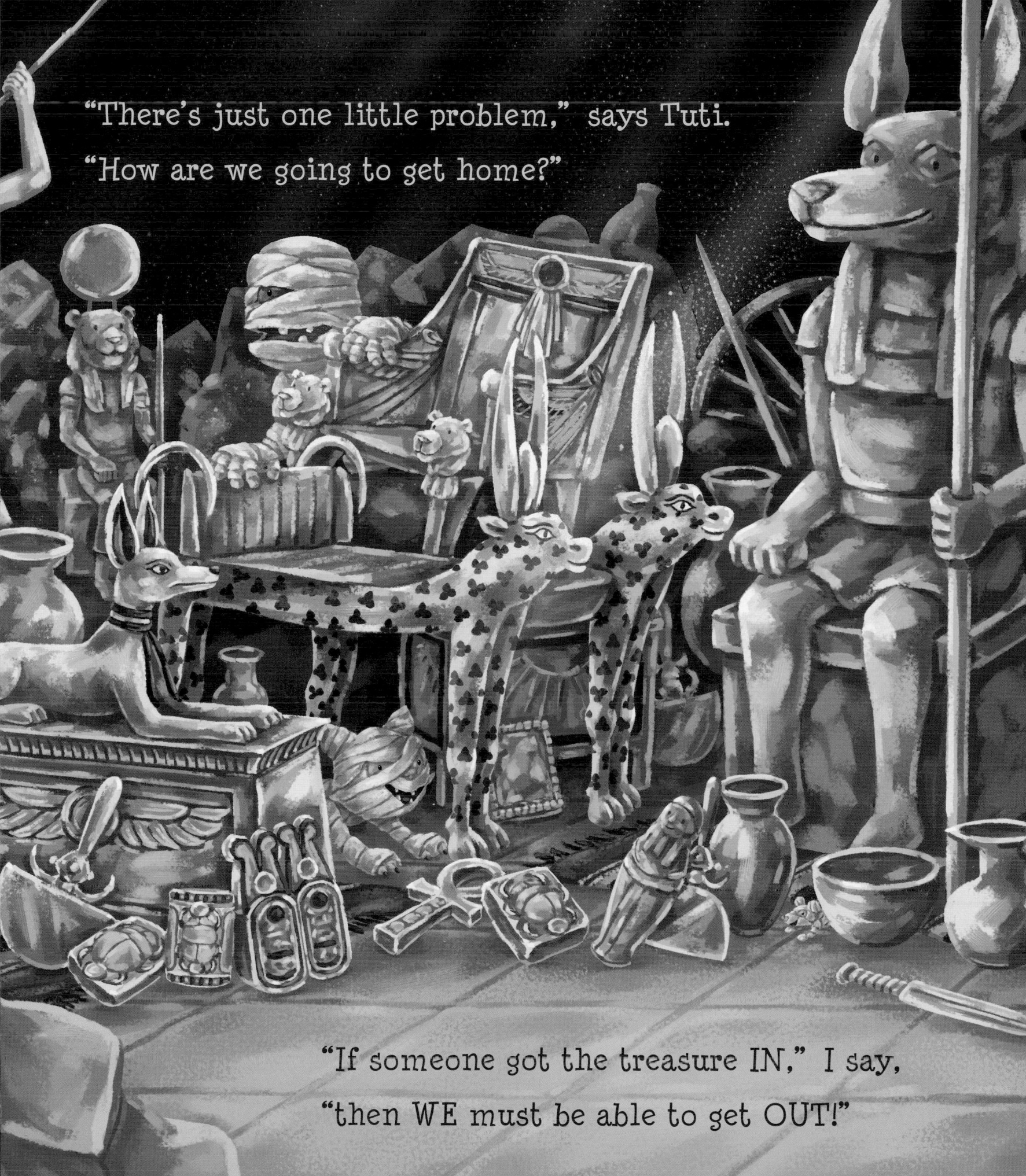

"There's just one little problem," says Tuti.

"How are we going to get home?"

"If someone got the treasure IN," I say,

"then WE must be able to get OUT!"

I spot a golden sarcophagus in the corner.

"Perhaps this guy can help," I laugh.

I pretend to shake his hand and . . .

DRUMBLE
RUMBLE
RUMBLE

The sarcophagus begins to open!

"Oh no!" cries Tuti. "The ghost of King Ra is coming to get us!"

"Wait here," says Anka. She disappears inside and the lid bangs shut!

"Anka! Noooo!" Tuti wails.

Nothing happens for a long time. Then . . .

"BOO!"

"Haha! Scared you!"
laughs Anka.

"Look Tuti," I say. "Anka's found the way out!"

Back at the palace, a delicious smell fills the air.
"Lunchtime – great!" cries Tuti. "I'm starving!"

I give my new friends a hug. "I'd better go,"
I say. "I think my lunch is ready, too."

"Thanks for helping us," says Anka.
"We'll tell our dad where the treasure
is so he can keep it safe forever."